P9-BBT-714

ANIMAL BABIES

By Bobbie Hamsa

Illustrated by Tom Dunnington

Children's Press®
A Division of Scholastic Inc.
New York • Toronto • London • Auckland • Sydney
Mexico City • New Delhi • Hong Kong
Danbury, Connecticut

Dear Parents/Educators,

Welcome to Rookie Ready to Learn. Each Rookie Reader in this series includes additional age-appropriate Let's Learn Together activity pages that help your young child to be better prepared when starting school.

Animal Babies offers opportunities for you and your child to talk about the important social/emotional skill of **natural curiosity**.

Here are early-learning skills you and your child will encounter in the *Animal Babies* Let's Learn Together pages:

• Vocabulary
• Maze: problem solving
• Naming numbers

We hope you enjoy sharing this delightful, enhanced reading experience with your early learner.

Library of Congress Cataloging-in-Publication Data

Hamsa, Bobbie.
   Animal babies/written by Bobbie Hamsa; illustrated by Tom Dunnington.

      p. cm. — (Rookie ready to learn)

ISBN 978-0-531-25640-4 (library binding) — ISBN 978-0-531-26800-1 (pbk.)

1. Animals—Infancy—Juvenile literature. I. Dunnington, Tom, ill. II. Title. III. Series.

   QL763.H36 2011   6591.3'9—dc22   2011010244

Acknowledgments
© 1985 Tom Dunnington, front and back cover illustrations, pages 3, 4, 6, 7, 9, 10, 12–16, 18, 20–22, 25–28, 30-37, 38 horse, barn, pig, 39–40. © iStockphoto/Thinkstock page 35.

A baby cat is a kitten.

A baby dog is a pup.

A baby deer is a fawn

until he's all grown up.

A baby pig is a piglet.

10

A baby horse is a foal.

A baby cow is a calf

until she's one year old.

A baby owl is an owlet.

A baby fish is a fry.

16

A baby kangaroo is a joey
until he's three feet high.

A baby rabbit is a bunny.

A baby bird is a chick.

A baby sheep is a lamb.

A baby beaver is a kit.

A baby lion is a cub.

(A baby bear is, too.)

A baby goat is a kid

and so are you!

Congratulations!

You just read about one sign of spring—*Animal Babies*—and you learned what each one is called.

About the Author

Bobbie Hamsa was born and raised in Nebraska and is the author of the popular series of books called Far-Fetched Pets. She lives in Omaha with her husband, Dick Sullivan, and children, John, Tracy, and Kenton.

About the Illustrator

Tom Dunnington has been an art instructor and illustrator for many years. In addition to illustrating books, Mr. Dunnington has created a series of paintings of endangered birds.

Animal Babies

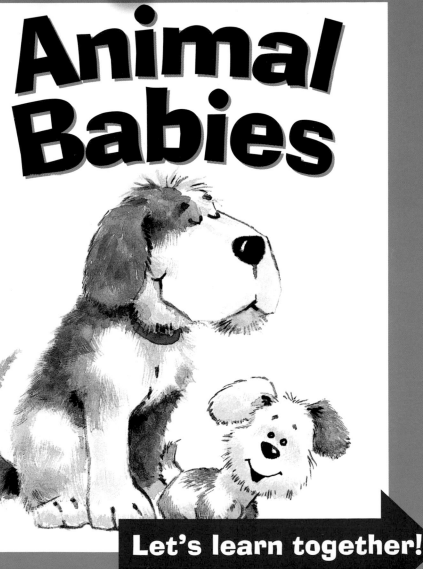

Let's learn together!

How Do We Know It Is Spring?

(Sing this song to the tune of "Row, Row, Row Your Boat.")

Spring, spring, spring is here.
Tell me how you know.
Ducks have ducklings, hens have chicks.
Baby animals start to grow.

Ladybugs and butterflies.
Rain falling on the pond.
Tadpoles growing into frogs;
Now that winter's gone.

Seeds, seeds, seeds, they sprout
flowers from the ground.
Leaves are growing on the trees.
Spring is all around.

PARENT TIP: Share this springtime song with your child. Then strengthen your child's language skills by going back through the story and talking about the different signs of spring she sees in *Animal Babies*.

34

Where's My Mom?

Many animal babies are born in spring.

Say the name of each animal baby. Then use your finger to match each parent to its baby.

kid

fawn

calf

mother cow

mother goat

mother deer

Celebrate Spring

Look closely!

You can see flowers, bunnies, and butterflies in spring.

- Find two **flowers** that look the same.
- Find two **bunnies** that look the same.
- Find two **butterflies** that look the same.

PARENT TIP: As you share this activity, you will be helping your child observe details in a picture and recognize similarities, important early literacy skills. Once your child finds the two identical butterflies, flowers, and bunnies in the scene, go back through the book. See if your child can find the bunny, butterfly, and flower in the story.

Take Me Home!

This little foal is lost. Help him find his barn. Use your finger to trace the path from the foal to the barn. Name the baby farm animal that is waiting at the barn.

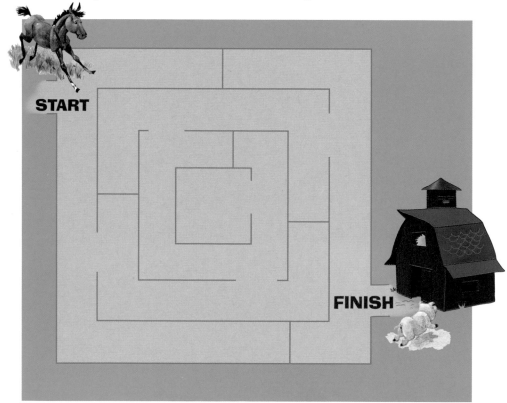

START

FINISH

PARENT TIP: Help your child build problem-solving skills, an important early math skill, by finding the path that will take the foal to the barn. Then go back through the story and talk with your child about the different animal homes pictured throughout the book.

Count Baby Animals

Say the numbers on the left. Then use your finger to match each number to the picture that shows that many.

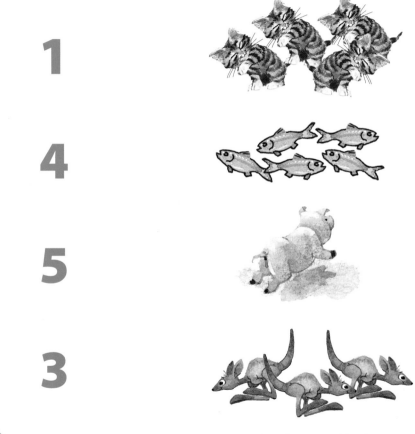

1

4

5

3

PARENT TIP: Support your child's skill in counting and number recognition, important early math skills, with this activity. After your child has matched the numbers to the baby animals, go back through the story. Have your child count the leaves on the twig the beaver is holding on the cover, the slipper on page 4, and the children on page 30.

39

Animal Babies Word List (51 Words)

a	cub	is	piglet
all	deer	joey	pup
and	dog	kangaroo	rabbit
are	fawn	kid	sheep
baby	feet	kit	she's
bear	fish	kitten	so
beaver	foal	lamb	three
bird	fry	lion	too
bunny	goat	old	until
calf	grown	one	up
cat	he's	owl	year
chick	high	owlet	you
cow	horse	pig	

▶ **PARENT TIPS:**

For Older Children or Readers:
Print the animal names from the word list on
individual index cards. Then go back through the
story and invite your child to find these animal
names in the story.

For Younger Children:
Point to the animal words on the list that start with
the letter *B*. Help your child identify the letter *B* that
begins each word, emphasizing the *B* sound as you
share each word. Then enjoy an "animal hunt" by
going back through the story with your child to find
each of these animals in the book.